The STARS CAME OUT on CHRISTMAS

By William Boniface
Illustrations by Stephen Waterhouse

PSS!
PRICE STERN SLOAN

One little star looked down upon the land.

Four little stars watched them settle in the hay.

Five little stars woke the cattle from their sleep.

Three little stars saw the strangers turned away.

Two little stars said: “The time is near at hand.”

Six little stars summoned shepherds and their sheep.

Seven little stars guided wise men by their light.

Eight little stars sensed the wonder in the night.

Nine little stars heard the sound of heaven's horn.